The
VERY LONG
Sleep

Polly Noakes

Bear, Chipmunk, Marmot
and Fox played all summer long.

"Wouldn't it be fun if we all lived together?" said Marmot.

"We would never be lonely," said Fox.

"Or bored," added Chipmunk.

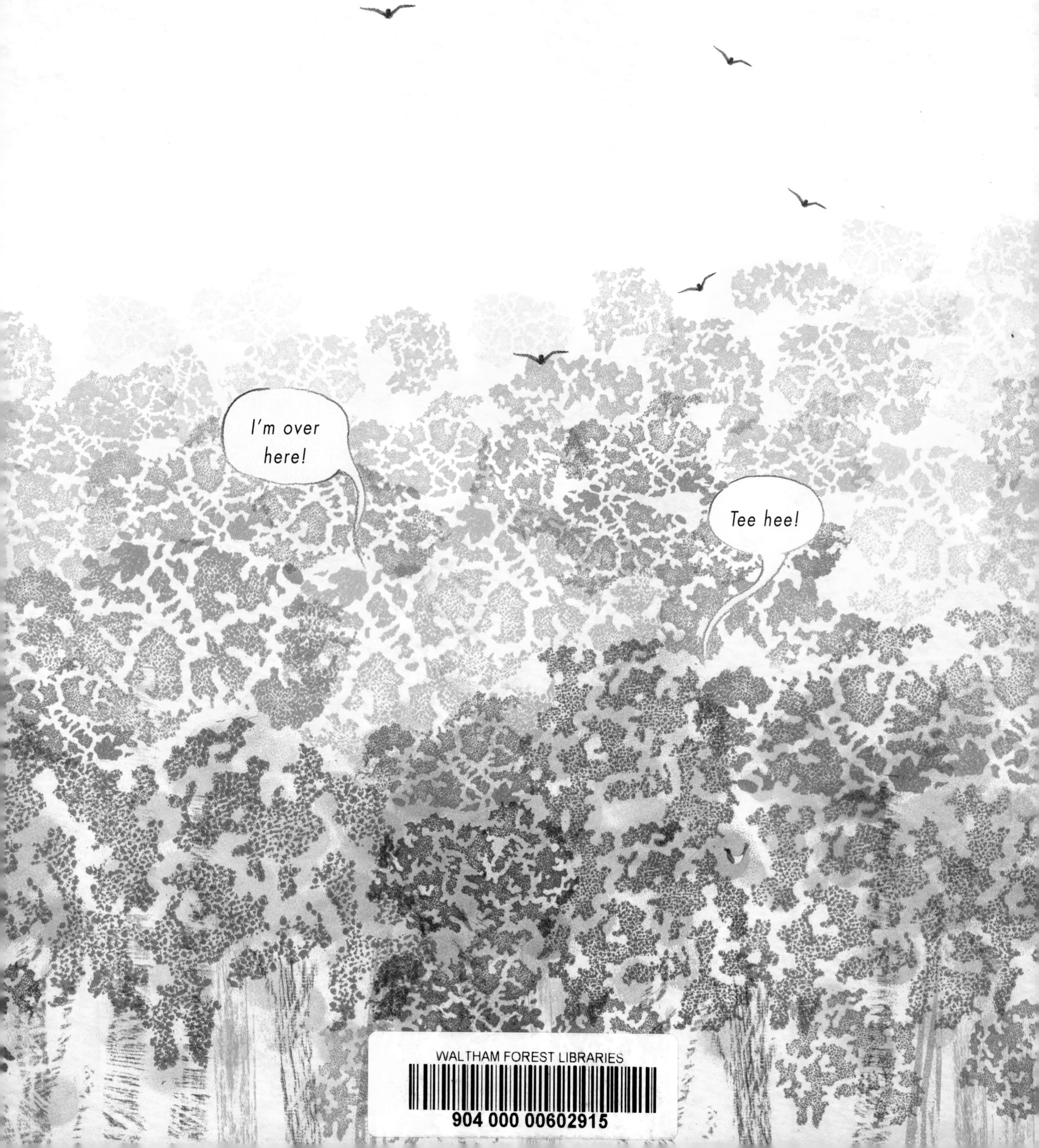
I'm over here!
Tee hee!

For my mother Kate,
who always inspired us to be creative

First published in 2017 by Child's Play (International) Ltd
Ashworth Road, Bridgemead, Swindon SN5 7YD, UK

Published in USA by Child's Play Inc
250 Minot Avenue, Auburn, Maine 04210

Distributed in Australia by Child's Play Australia Pty Ltd
Unit 10/20 Narabang Way, Belrose, Sydney, NSW 2085

Copyright © 2017 Polly Noakes
The moral rights of the author/illustrator have been asserted

ISBN 978-1-78628-128-9
CLP080817CPL10171289

Printed in Shenzhen, China

1 3 5 7 9 10 8 6 4 2

A catalogue record of this book
is available from the British Library

www.childs-play.com

They all agreed it was an excellent idea.
So they built a home tall enough, wide
enough and snug enough for them all.

It was perfect, except...

...Bear, Chipmunk and Marmot
forgot to tell Fox that when the frost came, they liked
to have a deep, deep sleep for a long, long time.

Every day Fox tried
to wake them up.

But no one stirred.

And every evening,
Fox prepared lots of food
in case they woke up.

But no one stirred.

Fox tried to sleep too,
but there was always
an itch that needed
scratching.

Fox was bored and lonely.

Life was very, very quiet.

Until...

Bang! Bang! **Bang!** **BANG!**

Bang! **Bang!** **BANG!**

Bang! **Bang!** **BANG!**

"Delivery for Chipmunk," cooed Pigeon.

"I will take care of it," said Fox.

A few weeks later there was a tap, tap, tap.

"Package for Marmot," puffed Pigeon.

"I will keep it safe," said Fox.
"Is there anything for me?"

"Not today," said Pigeon.

Weeks later they delivered an enormous box for Bear.

"I will be next! I will be next!" exclaimed Fox.
"And it will be the biggest package of them all!"

Fox waited and waited, but there was no knock on the door.

Fox was bored.

What could possibly be in the parcels?
Would it be very bad to take a little peek?

What on earth was that?

Ding DONG!

Ding DONG!

Ding DONG!

cuckoo!

Cuckoo!

CUCKOO!

RING-a-ling!

RING-a-ling!

RING-a-ling!

"Ahhh! Spring is here,"
yawned Bear.

"Thank goodness we didn't oversleep. I am SO hungry," added Marmot.

"It was a good idea to order alarm clocks," said Chipmunk.

"Where's Fox?" they all asked.

"Oh, there you are!" said Bear.

"Thank you for looking after our clocks,"
Chipmunk added.

"I am sorry I opened them," said Fox.

"And we are sorry we didn't tell you
that we hibernate in winter,"
said Marmot.

"At least I'll know for next year," said Fox.
"And maybe I can find another friend
who doesn't need a very long sleep!"